FLASH FORWARD
FAIRY*TALES

Snow White
AND THE Seven Dogs

A retelling by Cari Meister

Illustrated by Erica-Jane Waters

SCHOLASTIC INC.

For Marni, Samir, & all the doggies – C.M.

For Nick and Sienna – E.J.W.

ISBN 978-0-545-56569-1

12 11 10 9 8 7 6 5 4 3 2 1   14 15 16 17 18 19/0

Printed in the U.S.A.   40
First printing, September 2014

Designed by Maria Mercado

Once upon a time, there lived a girl with skin as white as snow. Her vain stepmother, the queen, gazed into a magic mirror day and night. "Mirror, Mirror on the wall, who's the fairest of them all?" Every day the mirror answered, "You, my queen, are the fairest by far."

In time, Snow White grew up. And when the queen asked the mirror who was the most beautiful, the answer was Snow White. The jealous queen sent Snow White into the forest, certain that she would die. Terrified, Snow White stumbled through the forest until she came upon seven friendly dwarves. But that was then. Flash forward to TODAY . . .

It was Sunday. The mall didn't open until noon. But Snow White and her stepmother were busy getting the shop ready.

"Snow!" yelled Evilyn. "Bring those boxes over here! Set out the shoes! Hang up the 'sale' sign!"

Even though Evilyn was mean, Snow loved working at the mall.

While Snow was busy, Evilyn rushed to the back room.

She fixed her hair. She put on some lipstick. After making sure that no one was watching, she flipped on the security monitor.

A screen flickered and a purple man appeared.

"Sheldon, Sheldon on the screen," said Evilyn, "who's the prettiest girl you've seen?"

Over the years, Sheldon's answer was always the same: "You are most beautiful, it's true. No one can compare with you."

Evilyn lived for this moment.

But today, Sheldon had a different answer.

"You are still beautiful, it's true. But Snow has grown more beautiful than you."

"Snow White?" Evilyn hissed. "That . . . that . . . that girl out there?"

Sheldon nodded.

"Ugh!" Evilyn threw a bottle of Purple Poison nail polish at the screen.

Snow poked her head into the room.

"Everything okay?" she asked sweetly.

Evilyn stared at her stepdaughter. She was beautiful. Jealousy grew over Evilyn's heart like a choking vine.

"Get lost!" she screamed. "And I don't mean for a little while, I mean FOREVER! I NEVER WANT TO SEE YOU AGAIN!"

Snow could not believe it. She ran outside. "Where should I go?" she cried.

To calm herself, she started to whistle. Suddenly, a mangy dog poked his head out from behind a trash can.

"Oh!" said Snow. "Hello, there!"

The dog gave Snow a big, wet kiss. He wagged his tail.

"Aren't you a cheerful pup!" she said. "I'll call you Happy."

Happy tugged Snow's sleeve. He pulled her toward a grooming shop. Then he ducked through the doggy door.

"Do you think anyone will mind if I come in?" asked Snow.

"Arf!" barked Happy.

Snow was greeted by six slobbery kisses. And one slobbery. . .

"Achoo!"

"Nice to meet you, Sneezy," said Snow.

Snow saw dogs of every shape and size! One snored in his bed. A grumpy little guy growled. And one huge dog hid behind a chair.

"It's okay, Bashful. You can come out," said Snow, patting the pup on the head.

Snow introduced herself. She told
the dogs all about Evilyn. They listened
closely. Well, all except Sleepy.

"I don't know what to do!" she cried.
Then she buried her face in Happy's fur.

"Oh my!" she said. "You need a bath! You all do! And haircuts. And your nails need trimming."

Snow spent the rest of the day cleaning up the seven dogs. Soon she had a new pack of best friends.

BASHFUL

SLEEPY

GRUMPY

HAPPY

DOPEY

SNEEZY

DOC

The next day, Evilyn turned on the security monitor.

"Sheldon, Sheldon on the screen," said Evilyn, "who's the prettiest girl you've seen?"

Sheldon cleared his throat. "You are beautiful, it's true. But Snow is still more beautiful than you."

"How can that be?" yelled Evilyn. "She isn't even here! Sheldon, show me Snow White."

Sheldon's screen flickered to show Snow happily dancing with the dogs.

As she stared at the screen, an evil smile spread across Evilyn's face. "I know just the thing to destroy her beauty!" she cackled.

Evilyn marched to the food court and ordered the biggest, sweetest smoothie she could find.

Then she added a secret potion.

"Soon Snow will turn ugly. Then I'll be the prettiest girl in town once more!" Evilyn laughed.

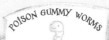

POISON GUMMY WORMS

Gruesome gummy worms—guaranteed to turn your enemies **UGLY**

"I can't wait to watch Snow's pure white skin wrinkle before my eyes!"

Evilyn put on a disguise and headed off to deliver her surprise.

Snow and the dogs were playing
"doggy in the middle" when there was
a knock at the door.

"Special delivery for Snow White,"
said Evilyn. "We're doing a taste test of
our new apple smoothie."

"That sounds delicious!" said Snow.
"I'll give it a try!"

The dogs could tell that Evilyn was a rotten apple. They growled and snapped. They barked and jumped.

"WHOA!" screamed Evilyn, losing her balance.

The smoothie fell out of her
hand. It landed on her face.

"My face!" screamed Evilyn. "My
beautiful face!"

After that, Evilyn was banned from the mall forever. She spent the rest of her days trying to come up with a cure for wrinkles.

And Snow White and the seven dogs? They lived happily ever after.